MY TEACHER for PRESIDENT

by Kay Winters

illustrated by Denise Brunkus

DUTTON CHILDREN'S BOOKS ★ NEW YORK

To Dr. Richard Creasey, a superintendent who encouraged and valued
the work of the teachers in the Palisades School District
K.W.

. . . and Linda Pratt for vice president!
D.B.

Library of Congress Cataloging-in-Publication Data

Winters, Kay.
My teacher for President/by Kay Winters; [illustrations by Denise Brunkus].—1st ed.   p. cm.
Summary: A second-grader writes a television station with reasons why his teacher would make a good
president, but only if she can continue teaching till the end of the year.
ISBN 0-525-47186-3
[1. Teachers—Fiction. 2. Schools—Fiction.] I. Brunkus, Denise, ill. II. Title.
PZ7.W767My 2004
[E] 2 22   2003019222

Published in the United States by Dutton Children's Books,
a division of Penguin Young Readers Group
345 Hudson Street, New York, New York 10014
www.penguin.com

Designed by Gloria Cheng

Manufactured in the U.S.A.

3 5 7 9 10 8 6 4

Dear Channel 39,

I saw on TV that elections are coming.

At school we have been learning about the president's job.

My teacher would be just right!

Let me know what you think.

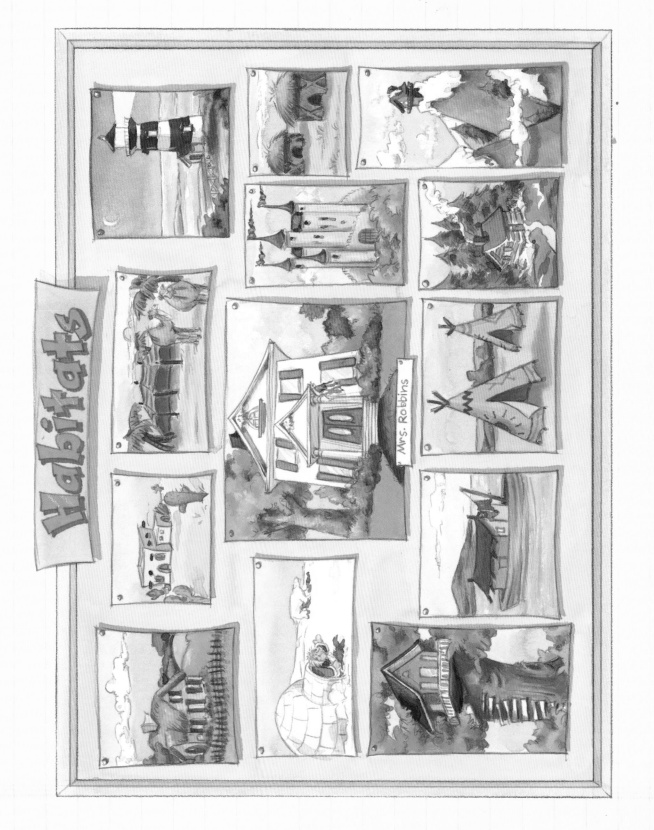

My teacher loves white houses.

She's used to being followed everywhere.

When my teacher walks into a room,
people pay attention.

My teacher goes to lots of meetings.

And she's always signing important papers.

My teacher acts quickly when there's an emergency.

And she says health care is important.

My teacher likes to go on trips.

President Robbins travels through Egypt.

President Robbins walks the Great Wall of China.

President Robbins enjoys Paris.

She deals with the media every day.

My teacher would be good for the country.

She wants to clean up the Earth.

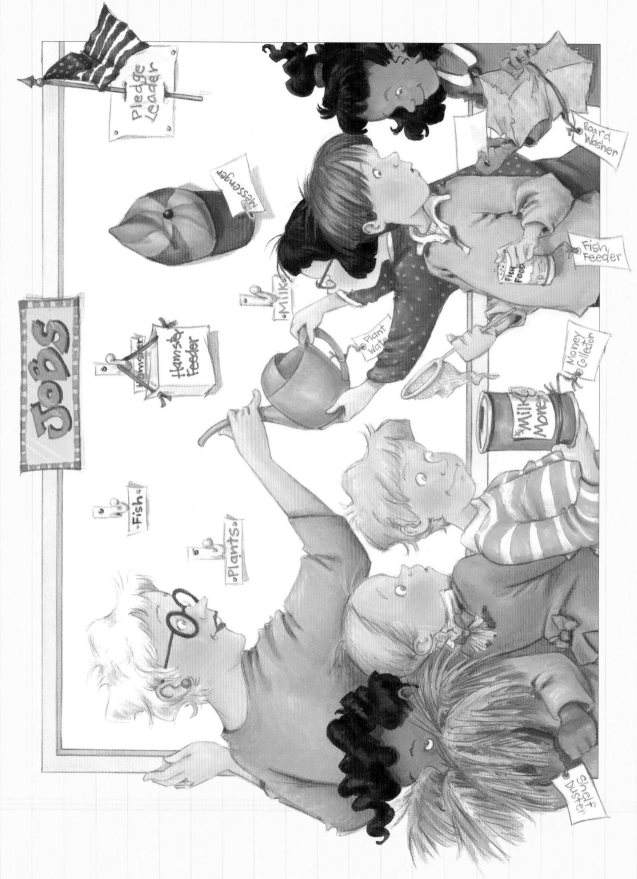

She finds jobs for people.

She is a good listener.

She believes in peace.

Love, Oliver

P.S. Just make sure she doesn't leave before the end of the year.